Nain Rouge

Keep your myths,

[signature]

by josef bastian

illustrations by bronwyn coveney

Honi soit qui mal y pense

"Evil be to those who Evil thinks"

Prologue.

Once upon a time, across the great sea, the kings and queens of Europe looked to knights, lords and ladies to maintain peace and balance in the land. People spoke of chivalry, a term used to describe what was best in all of us. Chivalry became the name for the general spirit or state of mind which inspired men and women to heroic actions, to greatness, keeping them in tune with all that was beautiful and sublime in the universe that expanded around them.

In the New World, the order of knights and chivalry died. In the New World, explorers and settlers came. They scrapped their old ways in exchange for adventure, discovery and opportunity. Decisions were made. Some of these decisions were good, and led to growth and prosperity for these strangers in a strange land. Some of their decisions were bad; and became buried in a dark history of war, strife and human conflict.

Now, the land and its people have grown up together. We are living in a land of democracy and personal freedom. We are living in a land where people had the right to vote, speak freely and protect themselves from danger. We are left to our own devices to choose between what is right and wrong, as long as we do not infringe upon people's rights in the process. The decisions started in our hearts and in our heads. In this land of individuals, we are left to decide between good and evil; to pursue our own happiness.

But in these current times, somewhere, somehow, something got lost, mixed up and out of balance. In this process of exploration and discovery, choices were made – some of them were bad.

Now we know that every bad choice, every dark thought, has to go somewhere. They build up over time and eventually manifest themselves in one fashion or another. Usually, this negativity creates nothing more than a bad mood, hurt feelings or a sad face. Fortunately, these things fade quickly and are soon forgotten.

But sometimes, evil does not go away. Sometimes the darkness builds up and up and up until it manifests into something quite astonishing, quite frightening and quite real.

This is where our story begins.

It is at these critical times, these times of crisis when we are forced to look deep inside ourselves, that we must ask...

"What do I believe in? What do I choose?"

Chapter 1. At the Museum

The museum felt very different today.

Elly and Tom both noticed it. These best friends had been to the Detroit Institute of Arts on field trips many, many times and had never felt such a creepy, eerie feeling. It was not quite a smell or a sound or something they saw. No, it was more like a whisper, a hint, a shadow, a feeling down deep in your soul that something was not quite right.

This tingling of uneasiness followed Elly and Tom from the main hall into the Diego Rivera Court. As they looked around,

Elly and Tom were swallowed up by the enormity of the scene that encircled them. Images of factories, pyramids, machinery, airplanes, gods and goddesses blurred past their eyes like a fast moving freight train. It was almost too much to take in at once. Fortunately, chairs and benches had been placed strategically around the room, so that their large group could settle in and unravel the activity that played so rapidly before them.

Some said that these *Detroit Industry* murals were the finest example of Mexican muralist work in the United States. Tom and Elly would not know whether to disagree or not. What they were about to learn, however, was that in 1932, Edsel Ford and Ford Motor Company commissioned Diego Rivera to create two magnificent paintings for the museum in its old Garden Court.

As they read the placards near the courtyard entrance, Elly and Tom learned that the north and south walls were devoted to three sets of images: the representation of the races of people that shape North American culture and made up its work force, the automobile industry, and the other industries of Detroit - medical, pharmaceutical, and chemical.
At the bottom of the walls were small panels which depicted the sequence of a day in the life of the workers at the Ford River Rouge plant.

The central panel of the north wall represented important operations in the production and manufacture of the engine and transmission of the 1932 Ford V8.

The major panel of the south wall was devoted to the production of the automobile's exterior.

Just as they finished reading the descriptions, their guide began her presentation about the Diego Rivera murals. Her voice echoed in the courtyard like a distant call from a far off hill. Elly and Tom barely understood a word of what she was saying. Instead, they swiveled their heads slowly around, like barn owls, trying to figure out the story that was being told within the giant symbols and pictures that covered every wall.

Elly's eyes would flash back and forth across the mural on the north wall. She could have sworn that there was a shadow moving, appearing and disappearing, shifting behind the industrial images and unfamiliar faces within the painting. She could catch a glimpse of it with her peripheral vision. But as soon as she would turn and focus, like a wisp of smoke, it was gone.

Then it happened. A resounding crash like none they had ever heard before. It came from the main gallery like a metallic ocean wave, clattering and clanking, crashing into the courtyard, soaking each visitor with the drowning noises of metal against metal against pewabic tile. It was so loud, Tom fell back in shock.

Instinctively, Elly ran back into the main hall, unafraid of the noise and commotion that was still emanating from that direction. As she burst into the room, she took about three steps and then froze in her tracks. The suits of armor that had so recently lined each side of the hall were in the process of falling, flying and slamming against each other. As the last armor fell, before the final echo faded, Elly saw something even more unbelievable.

At the far end of the hall where a 17th century Italian Corsaletto armor once stood, crouched a small, gnarled, bizarre-looking creature. His face was as red as new copper, rough, stubbled and twisted.

Tom came running in and caught up with Elly just in time to see this little man hopping up and down in an odd and joyful jig. He was surprised at the sight of this impish person, adorned in worn, threadbare clothes that looked like a blackish-brown animal pelt and a dingy greenish-gray mossy cap that was pulled down over the points of his ears.

This excited little creature that they watched dancing and jumping about seemed to be in a maddened frenzy of anger and joy. Just as Elly and Tom were taking in the entire scene, the little man stopped. The dancing stopped. The odd, queer, caterwauling sound he made stopped. Everything stopped - except his eyes.

As the echoes of falling armor had faded, the silent aftermath fell down around both children, like disturbed dust from an empty, unkempt room. Though still quite far away on the other side of the hall, his eyes never moved. He was staring right at them. They tried to look away from the piercing black eyes, but could not. The feeling that they had felt earlier in the day came over both of them – even stronger now.

It seemed like an eternity that he was gazing at them. He never moved. It was as if his dark, onyx eyes had caught them, trapped them in his stare. Slowly, his eyes changed like glowing embers caught by an arrant wind – coal black into deep blood red. It was then that this elfish man began to turn his head, slowly back and forth, ever so slightly, almost like he was tugging, trolling on the line of sight he had drawn between them. As his did this, both Elly and Tom began to feel dizzy, sick and nauseous. Dark and brooding thoughts began to bleed, seep into their brains.

Elly and Tom felt a strange spinning, as if they had been caught up in a vortex of darkness, sadness and despair. It was a feeling like rocking on the back legs of a chair, being pulled off-balance, bracing yourself for a fall and then being caught at the last second. Only the feeling wrapped around them again and again and again; like falling inside of your own fall.

On the verge of passing out, the children struggled to open their eyes once more. To their horror, they found that the little trollish figure was moving toward them. It may have been the dizziness or general disorientation, but both children watched as the man disappeared and re-appeared closer to them, like pieces cut away in a film strip and spliced back together, creating a strange, strobing effect. At the very moment the creature seemed to be upon them, Elly and Tom heard a loud, electrical POP, a queer cackling and then they dropped down, hard to the ground.

Everything went black.

Chapter 2. Bad Things

Faces hovered above Elly and Tom as light flooded back into their eyes.

"Are you guys OK?" came a voice from above.

As the children became more aware of their surroundings, they realized that they were lying flat on their backs in the main hall of the museum. Their teacher, Ms. Julian, was bent over them with a look of quiet concern, while some of the other children stood around Elly and Tom in a stunned semi-circle.

"Did anyone get the license plate number of that truck that

hit me?" Tom said as he slowly sat up and rubbed the back his head.

"What happened?" asked Elly as she pushed herself up off of the museum floor.

"We were hoping that you could tell us," said Ms. Julian.

Elly was the first to speak, "I'm not sure what happened, really. I ran in here when I heard all of the noise and the next thing I knew, I was knocked out cold."

Tom sat up a little bit more and added, "I was running in after Elly to see where she had gone. When I got into the main hall, I saw Elly staring at a p-"

Tom felt an elbow slam sharply into his rib cage.

"Ow, what did you do that for?!" Tom yelled as he turned toward Elly. Elly gave him a stern look, pursed her lips and shook her head ever so slightly, subtly telling Tom to keep his mouth shut.

"What I was saying," Tom began again, "Was that when I came in, I saw Elly staring at a pile of armor."

Tom looked back at Elly with the silent understanding that they would talk later in more detail about what the both of them had seen.

After the children were helped to their feet, Dr. Beele, the museum curator, entered the room - quietly approaching Tom and Elly amidst the broken armor and discarded weaponry. Dr. Beele was a world-renowned art historian and had been with the

Detroit Institute of Arts for many years. He was a very dapper man, always clean and pressed, with a dusty rose bowtie, salt and pepper hair, and antique Victorian glasses that seemed to balance perfectly at the end of his pointy, particular nose.

At first, Dr. Beele wanted to be sure that Elly and Tom were all right, which they were. Secondly, he wanted to reassure all the children that the museum was safe and that they could continue on with the rest of their tour. Lastly, Dr. Beele wanted permission from Ms. Julian to have a private conversation with both Elly and Tom. When Ms. Julian asked the children if they would mind going with Dr. Beele and joining up with the group later, Elly and Tom agreed.

Once the group had moved into another section of the museum, Dr. Beele smiled warmly at Elly and Tom, beckoning them to follow him to his private office. Dr. Beele walked with purpose and precision through the Detroit Institute of Arts, around artifacts, past the Taubman Wing, through medieval antiquities, down the spiral staircase and up into the private employee elevator to his corner office.

Dr. Beele's office appeared just as a world-traveling, highly-educated, cultured museum curator's office should appear. Ceiling to floor bookshelves filled with ancient historical texts and modern fictions surrounded a large, turn-of-century mahogany desk. Dotted about the room were various artifacts, paintings and figurines that served only to add to the powerful atmosphere of this broad-shouldered, academic workplace.

The intimidating effect of Dr. Beele's office was softened by a large, Italian Renaissance-styled window that made up the fourth wall of the room. These windows faced the western sky, just left of the main entrance of the museum, letting in the soft amber light of the afternoon sun. It was this combination of indirect light and expansive scenery that made the room both subtle and substantial at the same time. This western view from Dr. Beele's office drew in the center of the city. Between the large brick buildings and glass atriums that ran parallel down to Hart Plaza, was the main thoroughfare of the city of Detroit.

Woodward Avenue stretched right in front of the museum, marking the largest north/south gateway in and out of the city. Dr. Beele offered Elly and Tom a comfortable seat in two of his best red leather arm chairs. A silver tea service sat at the edge of his desk, already prepared with a special Darjeeling blend and miniature biscuits and cookies. After the curator poured them each a cup of piping hot tea, he turned toward the windows, staring briefing out at the Detroit Public Library directly across the street.

Beele finally turned to them and spoke, "Elly, Tom, you are probably wondering why I asked you to speak with me today. I must apologize for my haste in shepherding you up here so quickly."

The children shook their heads as if to say it was no trouble at all, when in actuality they would have found it very difficult to speak at that moment, with a mouthful of tea and lady fingers.

"I'll get straight to the point," Beele continued. "I know that you saw something today. I knew the moment I came into the hall and saw you both lying there. It is important that you know that this is not the first mishap to befall the museum as of late. In fact, these little disasters have been happening all over the city, and at an increasingly alarming rate, I might add."

Tom was the first to speak. "Well Dr. Beele, I can tell you what I saw. I came into the hall after Elly. Before I passed out, I caught a glimpse of a weird little man. I think he was the one who knocked down all of the armor."

Dr. Beele did not look surprised. In fact, he hardly even acknowledged what Tom was saying. "I know that you two had nothing to do with the damage to our collection," the curator replied; "I am more curious as to what you think you saw."

Elly finished swallowing her second macaroon and spoke up; "I'll tell you what I saw. I got a better look at him than Tom did. When I heard all that crashing, I ran into the main hall. When I looked around, I saw a gross-looking little red creature shoving armor against armor like a giant game of dominoes. He really seemed to be enjoying himself because he was laughing and dancing around the whole time."

"Yeah," Tom piped in, "he had this crazy laugh like a mix

between a cat, a hyena and a snake. It was kind of a high-pitched hissing laughter. Pretty creepy if you ask me."

Elly spoke up again, "Yes, but that was not the strangest thing. He saw us. He knew we were there. And when he looked at me, it was like I was frozen right where I stood. I could not move! The worst part of it all was the sick feeling I had the whole time he was staring at me. It was like he was tapping into all of the bad thoughts and feelings I had ever had and bringing them to the surface."

Tom shouted out, "Me too! That is exactly how I felt!"

It was clear that the children were becoming quite agitated, remembering the terrible experience that they had just been through. Dr. Beele quietly walked across the room in a calm, metered manner. He stepped toward the edge of his desk and offered Elly and Tom some more tea and cookies. Once the children had calmed down a bit, Dr. Beele went back to spot closer to the window.

"Tom, Elly," the curator began quietly, "There are some things you need to know about what you saw today. "
Both children slid back in their chairs, relaxing a bit but focusing all of their attention on the words that Dr. Beele was about to speak. The next two words that Elly and Tom would hear would change their lives forever. Two words that would echo in their heads, their hearts, for years to come.

"Nain Rouge," Dr. Beele stated simply.

"What? Who?" Tom blurted back.

"The Nain Rouge," the curator repeated.

Elly interrupted both of them, "I'm sorry Dr. Beele, but what is a Nain Rouge?"

The curator smiled apologetically and took a few steps toward them, "The Nain Rouge is the Red Dwarf."

Tom jumped back into the conversation, "OK, so what's a red dwarf? Don't tell me we were attacked by one of Snow White's rejects!"

Dr. Beele's face quickly became more serious as he moved toward Tom, slid the tea service aside and sat down on the edge of desk, directly in front of the children.

"Tom," Dr. Beele said earnestly, "this is nothing to joke about. The Nain Rouge is quite real and quite dangerous." The curator leaned in toward the children and began to tell them the story of what and who they had seen that day.

"The Nain Rouge is as old as the city itself, maybe older. Legend tells of a devilish creature whose appearance foreshadows terrible events within the city limits. The creature is said to have been attacked in 1701 by the first white settler of Detroit, Antoine de la Mothe Cadillac. Cadillac threw him out of the Fort Pontchartrain settlement, only to have the dwarf come back as a harbinger of doom. Ever since that time, Lutin has appeared in Detroit just before an impending disaster."

As Dr. Beele took a long breath, Elly interrupted, "Doctor, why did you call him Lutin?"

"Did I?" the curator quietly responded.

"Yes, you sure did," said Tom, chiming in. "Why did you say 'Lutin,' Dr. Beele?"

Dr. Beele got up slowly from the corner of the desk and made his way toward his shelves of books. Briefly stretching upon the balls of his feet, he pulled down a brittle-looking leather bound book from an upper shelf. The binding of the book creaked a little, as the curator opened to a dog-eared passage. Upon opening the book, a small blue-enameled medal object with a green ribbon fell from the pages to the floor. Tom reached over and picked it up gently.

"What is this?" Tom asked as he held the object. Now that it was closer to him, he could see that it was a medallion. It was the kind of medallion you would see pinned to the chest of a soldier or military officer. Within the medallion was an image of a knight on horseback, slaying a monstrous green dragon.

Tom handed the medallion to Elly so that she could see it too. Elly saw that there was an inscription in the medal. She looked it over and read it aloud:

"Honi soit qui mal y pense… what does that mean Dr. Beele?"

The curator smiled gently at Elly and softly beckoned for the medallion. Elly handed over the object to Dr. Beele quietly.

Once in his possession, Beele rolled the medallion over in his hands a few times, as if he were remembering something fondly from his past.

"Ah yes, the Most Noble Order of the Garter," Dr. Beele began. "I had almost forgotten that I still had this in my possession. If you must know, children, this medallion was given to me by a very special friend back when I was in England."

Elly interjected, "but the inscription and the knight and the dragon - what does it all mean?"

The curator looked at both children with reassurance, "The Most Noble Order of the Garter is nothing more than chivalrous order - a club of sorts. The knight on the medallion is St. George, the patron saint of England, famous for slaying an evil dragon.

"As for the saying, 'Honi soit qui mal y pense,' it is the motto of this order in Latin. It means 'evil be to those who evil thinks.'

"In more modern American English, one might say 'If you have evil in your heart and mind, it will eventually come back to you in some way, shape or form.'"

Elly spoke up again, "So, are you a knight?"

"A knight?" Dr. Beele repeated with a slight chuckle, "Well, I guess in a way I am. But that is neither here nor there, children. Though I do find it quite peculiar that you would find such an artifact at this point in time, we do have much more pressing matters to discuss. So, for now, let's set this topic aside and return to the issues at hand."

With that, the curator took one last curious look at the object, quietly slipped the medallion into his left breast pocket and picked up the ancient book again. Turning around toward the children, he leafed through pages and found the passage that he had been looking for. With only a brief pause, Dr. Beele began to read aloud,

"You are invisible when you like it; you cross in one moment the vast space of the universe; you rise without having wings; you go through the ground without dying; you penetrate the abysses of the sea without drowning; you enter everywhere, though the windows and the doors are closed; and, when you decide to, you can let yourself be seen in your natural form."

Upon finishing his reading, Beele closed the book and handed it to Elly. She took the book gently from his hands and held it so both she and Tom could see it. Across the leather cover, in flecked, faded gold was inscribed the title, *Le Prince Lutin*. The children looked back at Dr. Beele.

"Elly, Tom, you must understand, there are many things that I know. However, there are even more things of which I know nothing at all. The book you are holding is a French fairy tale, dating back to 1697. I discovered this book during one of my internships at the Louvre in Paris, France. There was a small roadside bookshop, just outside of the city. Something drew me to the shop and inexorably, to this book. It was not until today that I realized why I had purchased this quaint little story so many years ago. Now, things are being revealed that have been hidden for such a very long time, which only creates more questions for us all.

"From this story, I can tell you that Lutin is very powerful. He can go anywhere and take on any form that he likes. But he only shows himself in his "natural form" to those with whom he wishes to communicate.

"It is important that I share with you all that I know. Maybe you can help me find the missing pieces of the puzzle or at least help me understand the pieces we already have."

Dr. Beele paused for a brief moment and then began again: "There is a bit more information I can share. What I do know is that 'Lutin' is French, and has come to mean a mischievous hobgoblin or house spirit. However, the little creature you ran into seems to be Lutin himself; he has said so. And he is not mischievous, he is evil. Unfortunately, there is much more to Lutin than I will ever know."

Tom flopped back into his armchair, "Geez doc, every time we ask you a question, the answers get worse and worse! What do you mean he said so?"

"Remember that horrible hissing, crying sound you heard

just before you passed out? Well, that was Lutin calling out his own name. He wanted you both to hear it. The Nain Rouge's cry is heard only by those to which it is intended. For many are called but few are chosen."

"But why, Dr. Beele, why?" interjected Elly.

The curator paused for a little while, as if processing multiple volumes of thought in rapid succession. Elly and Tom waited for his answer for what seemed like an eternity. Finally, the doctor took a deep, cleansing breath and softly said to both children,

"Because you have been chosen."

Chapter 3. The Chosen

Elly and Tom felt dizzy again. Dr. Beele's words wafted through their ears, encircling their thoughts like the heavy perfumed smoke of an overpacked hookah pipe. The rest of the conversation with the curator blurred into nothingness. Before Elly and Tom knew it, they were back with their group from Royal Oak Middle School, heading for the school bus that would take them back north, out of the city.

The yellow bluebird school bus turned right onto Woodward Avenue and crossed back in front of the main entrance of the Detroit Institute of Arts. Elly and Tom had found a seat toward the back of the bus and slid close to each other, whispering quietly about the day they had just experienced. The bus made a slight detour off of the main street, avoiding the asphalt trucks and paving crews that routinely filled the ever-expanding ruts and potholes that dotted so many of the city's roads.

The children paused for a moment, looking up from their conversation, they noticed the new route the school bus had taken. As they looked out the bus window, they could see the Detroit Mounted Police station roll slowly past the side of their bus. How strange it was to see horses, barns and stables right in the middle of concrete, glass and cement. That familiar barnyard smell of hay, leather and manure seemed quite out of place in this bustling, urban environment.

Elly and Tom began to relax a little bit. They could feel their back and shoulder muscles release as their conversation faded into silence and they slid gently back onto the green vinyl seats of Row 24 on the right side of the bus. Maybe this had all been a dream or a figment of their collective imaginations.

As the bus completed its detour, it turned left to head back onto Woodward Avenue. Like the tail end of a yellow python, the rear of the bus slid quietly past the corner of the stables at the mounted police station. Without really thinking, both Elly and Tom peered out of the window at a broad-backed black stallion, roped to the white wooden fence at the edge of the stable.

The horse looked up from its bale of hay and stared right

at them. Its eyes were as black as night and twice as deep. Elly gripped Tom's hand.

"Do you see that?" she whispered.

"I see it, I see it," Tom hissed back between his clenched teeth.

The dark horse never broke his gaze at the children. Elly and Tom were frozen in fear and fascination; like watching a car accident happen in slow motion right before your eyes. Elly squeezed Tom's hand even harder. The horse was smiling at them. It was not a friendly smile. Actually, it was less of smile and more of grin; an evil grin. They had seen those eyes before. They had seen that grin before too. Without really knowing, Tom pulled Elly closer. It was Lutin. He was watching them and they could feel it. They could feel it within every muscle, every bone, and every sinew of their bodies.

The bus bumped and jumbled back onto Woodward Avenue. Elly and Tom were still clutching each other, though no one else really noticed. As the heavy transmission clunked into third gear, the bus lurched forward, gaining a bit more speed as it went.

Elly turned quietly to Tom and softly said, so close that no one would hear, "Why us?"

Chapter 4. *Fast Friends*

***E**lly and Tom* had grown up together in the mid-sized suburb of Royal Oak. Royal Oak was incorporated as a city in 1921, but its name was much older. As far back as 1819, Michigan Governor Lewis Cass and several companions set out on an exploration of Michigan territory to disprove land surveyors' claims that the territory was swampy and uninhabitable. On their journey, they encountered a stately oak tree with a trunk considerably wider than most other oaks. Its large branches reminded Cass of the legend of the Royal Oak tree, under which King Charles II of England took sanctuary from enemy forces in

1660. Cass and his companions christened the tree the "Royal Oak." And so the city received its name.

Oddly enough, the original "Royal Oak" tree was destroyed by a strange, unexpected storm that came up from the south, from Detroit actually, many years ago…

Now, Royal Oak was the kind of place where people loved to live. The tree-lined streets, sturdy homes and quaint downtown area seemed to lift you just out of reach of the big city problems. Yet, whenever anything bad happened in Detroit, its effects still reverberated out and up to Royal Oak, where the people would discuss matters quietly, in private. There was always a sense of silent thankfulness and uneasiness with the citizens of Royal Oak: they were thankful that the growing problems were not theirs, and uneasy that the negative vibrations were coming north, with increasing strength and frequency.

Elly and Tom had lived in Royal Oak all of their lives.

Elly Williams had always been above average. In fact, one might call her an overachiever – in everything. Elly excelled in volleyball, tennis, track, mathematics, debate, English composition and language arts – just to name a few items on her long list of accomplishments. Despite her high achievements, though, Elly often appeared shy and slightly hesitant. There seemed to be an insecure energy about her that constantly drove her to achieve and excel at everything she attempted. It was as if she was being chased by the shadow of her true self, hiding behind the movement and activity until the dark shade passed by her unnoticed. The awards and accolades from her teachers and peers became a useful smoke screen to camouflage the fear and doubt that flowed so subtlely, just below the surface of her thinly-veiled anxiety.

Tom Demine was aware of all of this. Well, actually, he had never really thought too much about Elly and her "emotions." Tom just knew Elly, inside and out. They had grown up together on Cedar Hill and been in school together since kindergarten. Tom was the kind of boy that let his actions speak loudly, instead of his words. He was not much of a talker; he was really more of doer. As far as Elly went, Tom was never that impressed with all of Elly's medals, certificates or awards. In his mind, those were just ways of other people telling you how great you were. Tom didn't need any of that stuff. He was confident in himself. He could do just about anything he put his mind to do. The trick with Tom was actually being able to put his mind to do anything.

Tom was a scatter-brained, free spirit who was often known to leap before he ever thought to look. That is why Tom was always getting into some sort of mischief. Oh, he never did anything really bad, just little things, like rolling smoke bombs down the hall on the last day of school, missing some of his class assignments, or forgetting to shut the water off when filling the neighbor's swimming pool (flooding their backyard and basement in the process). If they were giving out awards for forgetfulness and bad judgment, Tom would have more medals and trophies than Elly.

Maybe this was why Elly and Tom got along so well. Tom had the confidence that Elly was lacking, while Elly had the discipline of thought that Tom needed to get anything done. The fact that they had been together for so long, allowed them to communicate instinctively, often without ever speaking.

As the pair got older and moved into middle school, they both learned to keep their special relationship under wraps. A few kids had made comments about them being "lovebirds" or a "cute couple," so they were always careful about how much time they spent together during school hours. Other than that though, Elly and Tom were inseparable. There was always a comfortable understanding that flowed between them, allowing them to communicate open and freely without ever having to explain too much.

During this time of confusion and mystery, it was a good thing that Elly and Tom were in this predicament together. For some reason, they both felt that if something bad was going to happen, it would be better if it happened to them both - together. After all, misery does love company.

S*ince it had* been an all-day field trip, the children had only a few minutes to gather their things from their lockers before the final dismissal bell rang. Tom told Elly to meet him after school in the library media center, so that they could figure out what was really going on.

The media center was a great place to meet. There were always after school activities going on, so on most days, the center was open for a few hours after school. Elly entered the room and found Tom already sitting in the computer lab.

"Elly, get in here, you've got to see this," Tom called out from behind the flat screen computer monitor.

"I thought we were going to talk, not play games on the computer, "Elly sighed in frustration, as she pulled up an extra chair and sat next to Tom.

Tom replied indignantly, "I'm not playing games. I am doing research on the Nain Rouge, and look what I found. Remember, Dr. Beele said that the little monster was thrown out of Fort Pontchartrain over 300 years ago."

"So, big deal, we already knew that," Elly said.

"Yeah, but did you know that Fort Pontchartrain was also known as Fort Detroit, which is where the city actually started?"

Elly leaned in closer to the computer monitor, "OK, you've got my attention now. What else?"

"Here," Tom continued. "Remember when we did that genealogy project in school last year? And you and I found out that we were related way, way back, many generations ago?"

Elly rolled her eyes, "Yeah, how could I forget? I'm still trying to get over the 'Kissing Cousins' nickname everyone slapped on us."

"Well get over it El, I did. Anyway, do you remember who our common ancestor was? It was Marianne de Tonty!"

Elly gave Tom a disconcerted stare, "So, what of it? I don't even know who that is."

Tom gently put his hand on the back of Elly's head and pushed her closer to the computer screen.

"Here, read this," he said firmly.

Elly looked at the web site on the monitor and silently read,

"Pierre Alphonse de Tonty was born in 1659 to Laurent and Angelique (de Liette) de Tonty. Some time after 1689 and before 1701, Tonty married Marianne la Marque, daughter of Francois la Marque. This was Marianne's third marriage.

Tonty was the Captain of Cadillac's party which founded Fort Pontchartrain du Detroit in 1701. He was a loyal, trusted officer. He was known to the Native Americans as "the man with the iron hand" due to an artificial limb."

"Ok, I get it, "Elly said after a time, "We're related to Marianne de Tonty, so what's the big deal?"

"The big deal is that her husband was an officer in Cadillac's expedition. He helped found Fort Pontchartrain!"

Elly paused for a minute and let all of this information sink in. She now knew that Tom and she were directly linked to the original French settlers. The blood of their ancestors now ran through their veins.

After a few minutes, she leaned back her chair and pointed directly at Tom.

"I bet this is why we were chosen. Something must have happened with the Nain Rouge back then and since we are related to these first settlers, we have to pay the price!"

The gravity of this moment soon settled on both Elly and Tom like a damp, woolen blanket. For the first time, they realized that what had happened that day was just the tip of the iceberg. There was much more going on around them than what appeared to the naked eye. It was as if an invisible storm was beginning to swirl around them, creating a vortex of energy, information and strange history that was growing in its intensity. They were now mixed up with forces dark and sinister that were not going to go away easily.

Eventually, Elly and Tom became filled with a sense of urgency. They knew that something was not right and they were the ones who were going to have to fix it.

"We need to find a way to contact Dr. Beele," Elly stated. "He is the one person who can help us."

"Yeah, but how are we going to get all the way back down to Detroit without someone asking us a bunch of questions?" Tom quipped back.

"Well, we will just have to find a way," Elly snapped back. "We can't afford to wait too long. I'm just afraid that something else bad will happen if we don't do something right now!"

"Um, I could steal the principal's car and we could drive down there right now, if you want," Tom coolly suggested.

Elly gave Tom a piercing, daggered look.

"OK El, geez, I was just kidding, lighten up…" Tom tried to smooth things over; "Let's talk to our parents and see if they will give us a ride down this weekend. We can tell them we have to do research for a paper or something."

Elly's stare mellowed into a more contented look, "Well, now you are back on track. That sounds like an idea we can make happen. I will start working on my mom and dad tonight."

"Great," Tom said, "I'll see what I can do when I get home too."

"Awesome," Elly said, sounding a bit more satisfied, "I'm sure that Dr. Beele will be anxious to learn what we've discovered. This could be the big clue we're looking for."

Hieronymus **Stanley Beele** was born in Johannesburg, South Africa, to American missionary parents. After being born, he relaxed quietly in a modest clay-brick home just above the bustling city for his first week on this earth, and has been traveling and adventuring ever since.

Hieronymus's childhood consisted of attending various International American schools around the world. He spent months on end in England, Switzerland, Greece, Hungary, Finland, Nepal, China, Borneo, Russia, Brazil, Chile, Costa Rica and even Easter Island.

As a boy, he learned to be inquisitive and resourceful, making friends easily and assimilating quickly into myriad cultures, in which he was constantly being dropped. He had more adventures as a boy than most people have in an entire lifetime. He had zip-lined through the Costa Rican rainforest, climbed the Acropolis of Athens and even set up base camp at the foot of Mt. Everest. All of this before he had reached the ripe old age of sixteen.

At the age of seventeen, he attended Corpus Christi College at the University of Oxford, England. It was there that he gained his appreciation for fine art and literature, earning dual doctorate degrees in European Art History and Medieval Folklore.

Yet, despite all of these high adventures and the great learning that was achieved during the first twenty-plus years of his life, Hieronymus Stanley Beele felt quite alone in the world. It seems that with all his activities and moving about, he never allowed himself to dig his roots down too deep in any one place. After lengthy conversations in Oxford pubs or long lectures about Renaissance art, he often found himself walking down High Street alone, heading toward his bland, gray upper flat which he rented for just a few pounds a week.

It was not until he returned to his homeland in the United States that he really began to connect with people instead of places. After his study at Oxford, he interned at the Metropolitan Museum of Art in New York City. His internship consisted of working with school groups and assisting teachers and students in the discovery of European Art from the Middle Ages to the present time.

As an intern at the Metropolitan, he discovered the joy of sharing his rich subject matter expertise with each young visitor to the museum. In return, he built many new friendships with both teachers and students, creating special bonds that would continue to grow and blossom for years to come.

Eventually he completed his education and became Dr. Beele, his internships growing into full-time positions. Even so, he moved around the United States, taking various assistant and then director positions in Atlanta, Cleveland, Miami, Phoenix, Portland and eventually Detroit. As the curator of the Detroit Institute of Arts, he found true happiness and harmony. His role as chief administrator of the DIA allowed him to maintain close contact with the public, while still being able focus on his love of art.

It was not until the strange happenings began within the walls of the museum that Dr. Beele started to see that he had signed up for more than he originally bargained for in his curator employment contract.

Initially, he thought that all the commotion would settle down; perhaps just go away on its own. But it didn't. The Nain Rouge was getting stronger. He could feel it deep down in his compassionate and introspective heart.

And now, there were children involved. In all of his travels and adventures, he had never felt as much anxiety and consternation as he felt at this moment. This situation was no longer just about him and his museum. It was about the lives of two young people, the city, the surrounding region and all of its inhabitants.

The sudden gravity and weight of the world around him settled down upon the shoulders of Doctor Hieronymus Stanley Beele. For the first time in his life he did not know what he was going to do next.

Chapter **7.** *Answers and Questions*

***T**he next two* days passed in a fog of mundane repetition. Elly and Tom went through their daily routines with robotic precision, not wanting to let anyone know what they had learned. They walked through their daily classes in a sort of a murky haze. When their friends asked what was wrong, they would just make up an excuse about not feeling well or that they were worrying about some upcoming exams.

Though on the outside, Tom and Elly appeared sluggish and disinterested, inside, their minds were racing with rapid conjecture and anticipation, wondering what was going to happen next.

Friday finally came with the hopes that they would be able to get back down into the city to see Dr. Beele. By Friday afternoon, Elly learned that their hopes would be realized. But the news was bittersweet.

Elly came home from school to find her mom and dad sitting at the kitchen table. She knew right away that something was very wrong.

Her dad worked at Compuware in downtown Detroit. He was in the Campus Martius building in the heart of the city. Elly's dad never got home this early from work, never.

"Honey, can we talk to you for a minute?" Elly's mom called to her from the kitchen.

"Sure mom, just a minute." Elly took off her shoes and jacket slowly, in anticipation of the bad news that she just knew was headed her way.

Elly came over and sat down next to her mom at the table.

Her dad was the first to speak. "Sweetie, I got some bad news from work today…"

Elly could see that her dad was starting to get choked up. His eyes began to water a little bit and his voice seemed to get caught in his throat. She thought she could break the tension by saying something, anything:

"Dad, don't worry. Whatever it is, I can take it, really…"

Unfortunately, Elly's words only served to get her dad more upset. Despite his sadness, he spoke up again,

"Well, I just let your mom know that I was let go from my job. We thought you should know too. This was my last week."

For some reason, these words seemed to hang in the air after her dad spoke them. For a brief, awkward moment, no one knew what to say. Finally, Elly's dad spoke again. "They said that I can come back and clean my desk out on Saturday. I guess they want to save me the embarrassment of having to face everyone at the office. At least they left me some dignity, I guess."

Her dad got quiet again, as if he was going to lose it entirely. But he didn't cry. He just sat back and stared ahead, focusing on nothing but the silence and emptiness of their blank kitchen wall and the mute, shocked faces of Elly and her mom.

A lot of people were getting laid off. Not just from Compuware, but all around the Detroit area. Houses were not selling. Cars and trucks were not selling. The banks were failing. It seemed as if the threads of society were loosening around the entire region, unraveling the very fabric of the region and dismantling people's lives. Now her dad was out of work and Elly was experiencing firsthand the sadness and despair that was sprouting up all around her.

Later that night Elly called Tom and broke the sad news to him. Tom could really understand, since his mom had been let go from General Motors only one month before.

The only good news was that they now had a way to get back down to the Detroit Institute of Arts to talk to Dr. Beele. Elly and Tom would ride down with her dad and he would drop them off while he settled his final affairs at his old office.

Saturday morning greeted Elly and Tom with a gray, drizzly reception. Neither of them had slept very well the night before and the bland morning air did little to lift their spirits. After a light breakfast, the children got into Elly's dad's car and headed down Woodward toward to their respective destinations.

The ride into Detroit was very strange. The clouds seemed to hang a bit lower as the expedition party approached Eight Mile Road; the city limits. Upon crossing over into the city, Elly and Tom noticed that quirky, unsettling feeling coming over them again. Simultaneously, the children began to taste the bitter, smoky flavor of burnt ashes in their mouths. Their noses picked up a faint whiff of brimstone and the rotting stench of landfill.

"I think I'm going to be sick," Tom groaned as he held his stomach.

"Don't," Elly warned, "that's just what he wants from us. He is trying to stop us from getting any farther. He knows we're on to something."

Tom heeded Elly's warning and convinced himself out of asking Mr. Williams to stop the car. The clouds slid lower on the horizon and the day grew darker and more ominous as the children quietly endured the last few miles of the journey to the museum.

The Ford Explorer pulled up in front of the Detroit Institute of Arts.

Elly's dad turned toward the children in the back seat, "OK kids, I'll see you in a few hours. I pick you up right here. Call me on my cell if you have any problems."

They both thanked Mr. Williams, slamming the car door as they stepped up on the curb. Elly and Tom walked past the Auguste Rodin's *Thinker* statue, on their way into the museum. They paused for a moment, looking up at the large bronze man, frozen in deep contemplation. There was a troubled, confused feeling that seemed to emanate from the statue. Then, without warning, the metal giant moved. His back straightened and his shoulders were drawn back, as his cold heavy hand released itself from under his chin. Before Elly and Tom could yell, scream or even utter a word, "the Thinker" stood up and pointed an enormous index finger directly down upon them. A wicked, evil sneer drew across his heavy face. Then the sound came. That horrible, nails-against-the-chalkboard sound.

Lutin was beckoning them. He was speaking his own name. The children ran. Out of fear and instinct, they ran up the many steps of the museum and yanked open the thick, brass doors

with unusual ease, stumbling in to the main hall of the Detroit
Institute of Arts.

Dr. Beele was just inside the doors, ready to greet Elly and Tom.

"Did you see that?!" yelled Tom at Dr. Beele, as he regained his breath and balance.

"If you are asking whether or not I saw you and Elly blow through my museum doors like a rogue tornado, then the answer is yes, I did see that."

"No," Elly interjected; "Tom was asking if you saw the statue, it was the Nain Rouge! It is after us!"

A look of great concern came over the curator's brow. He

went over to one of the brass doors, opened it and looked out at *The Thinker*. The statue was still there, where it always had been; sitting in its thoughtful pose, staring out upon Woodward Avenue in perpetual rumination.

Dr. Beele turned back away from the door and looked at Elly and Tom. He could see that they were very upset and quite frightened. Forcing a slight smile and a warm, reassuring touch on their shoulders, he said, "Come with me."

With that, Dr. Beele escorted the children up to his office. The familiar room seemed less intimidating than before, and Elly and Tom were happy to see that the cookies and tea had been refreshed since their last visit. Both children quietly took their assigned seats in the squeaky leather arm chairs, as the curator poured them each a cup of Earl Grey.

Tom was the first to speak, "Doctor, you would not believe the things we have seen since we talked to you the last time."

Elly added, "It's as if the Nain Rouge is following us. Like he wants something from us."

The curator had pulled up an extra arm chair and was sitting directly across from the children now.

"Elly… Tom… Remember I told when we first met that there are many things I know and many more things of which I know nothing? Well, Lutin is one creature that falls deeper into my 'not-knowing' category."

Tom spoke up again, "Well, there are a few things Elly and

I can share with you that may help. Last year, we learned that we were both related to Marianne de Tonty. We just found out this week that she was married to one of the captains at Fort Pontchartrain."

The curator's eyes widened, "Is that so? Well, this is very interesting, very interesting, indeed. She was married to the man with iron hand…"

Elly looked at him, puzzled, "How did you know that, Dr. Beele? We read on the internet that the Native Americans called her husband, Pierre, that name because he had an artificial hand."

"Yes," Dr. Beele acknowledged, "And do you know how he lost that hand?"

Both children replied in unison, "No."

Dr. Beele took a deep sigh, sat back in his chair and calmly spoke the word, "Lutin."

After a period of stunned silence, the curator went to explain the entire story, as he had heard it:

"It seems that during the founding of the Fort Pontchartrain, Cadillac and his expedition had made a deal with the Native Americans to settle certain tracts of land near the river. The natives had warned Cadillac about the Nain Rouge. They had told him that this creature was part of the land and needed to be appeased in order that the settlers might work and farm the land in peace.

"Cadillac brushed away their warnings as silly, primitive superstitions and allowed his people to begin building houses, plowing fields, and planting crops. After a short while, the settlers began to notice that some of their livestock was missing. Then, crops began to dry up and wither without warning or reason. In short, the settlement was failing.

"One evening, when Cadillac and his some his officers were in their cabin, they heard a mournful, terrible cry outside their door. Upon opening the door, they looked down upon a small, little man, no higher than a yard stick.

"The tiny stranger stepped inside the cabin and introduced himself as 'Lutin: the Steward of the Straits.' Lutin was very cordial and friendly. In fact, he made it clear that he wanted to work with the settlers to build a great city upon his spot in the wilderness. He was willing to share his knowledge of the land, the flora, the fauna, its people and everything around them. It was at that point in the conversation that things turned ugly. Cadillac and his men laughed at the little man. They mocked him and called him a fool. They stated quite clearly that they would take whatever they wanted, whenever they wanted, from whoever they wanted.

"At this, the slight stranger began hopping and jumping up and down. His once pink-peach skin turned an angry, hot red. His fingernails manifested into claws and his face gnarled up into contorted knots.

"One of Cadillac's officers, Pierre de Tonty, reached out to subdue the creature and was bitten most fiercely upon his left hand.

"A great commotion ensued and Lutin escaped. But before he did, he hissed out these parting words,

Keep what you steal and steal what you keep

The shepherd must pay for his sins with his sheep.

"Now, ever since that fateful night, Lutin has appeared just before any disaster befalls the city of Detroit."

The curator stopped, a bit winded, and caught his breath before he spoke again. He took a gentle sip of his tea and looked softly back at Elly and Tom, "it all makes sense now. The story goes on to say that Pierre de Tonty lost his mangled hand after the bite the Nain Rouge had given him became infected. The curse that Lutin uttered before he disappeared has been cast upon both of your families.

"I am afraid to tell you, that you two are the sheep that Lutin was talking about. This curse is your legacy."

E*lly's cell phone* rang just as the bomb that Dr. Beele had dropped went off. Tom was sitting next to Elly in a sort of motionless, stunned stupor. Elly's dad was on the phone. He wanted the kids to walk a few blocks over to his office. He had gotten tied up in some clean-up issues at work and planned on meeting them down at the Hard Rock Café for lunch.

Elly hung up the phone just as Tom began to mumble, "D-D-Dr. Beele? What does all this mean for us? I mean, for Elly and me?"

The curator got up from his chair and began to pace slowly and softly around the room.

"As I told you two when we first met, there are things I know and things I do not know. This I do know; you are the heirs to stolen land; the land upon which this entire city was built. Lutin seems to believe that there is a debt that remains unpaid and you two are the debtors.

"Now, that explains the 'why you' question. But what I fail to understand is the "why now" question. Why would Lutin want to call in his marker now?"

Beele stroked his chin repeatedly, puzzling over this question. It was clear that life in Detroit was getting progressively worse. Economic woes, people losing their jobs, political corruption and a professional football team that had not won a championship since 1957!

Tom asked an even more pointed question, " So how are we supposed to pay back a debt that some distant relatives owed 300 years ago?"

In his gravest and most somber tone yet, Beele spoke softly to Elly and Tom, "That, I'm afraid, you will have to ask Lutin himself."

"Ask him himself? "Elly quipped. "And where are we supposed to find him? He seems to be everywhere and nowhere at the same time."

Beele replied, "I suspect that in his own good time, he will find you."

With heavy hearts and spinning heads, Elly and Tom thanked the curator and made their way out of the museum and down Woodward toward Campus Martius. Both children walked south down the avenue in a heightened stupor, both acutely aware, yet unaware of the city that wrapped around them as they walked.

Neither child knew whether or not Lutin would jump out and attack either of them on the spot. It would almost be better if it had happened that way. It was the anticipation of not knowing that was killing them. He was the predator. They were the prey. There were too many places to hide; too many shadows to camouflage the evil that they knew was watching, waiting in the urban jungle in which they traveled.

Hostile, aggravated thoughts had a way of quickening one's pace along city sidewalks. Elly and Tom had every reason to move with swiftness and determination toward the Compuware Building. On the streets, it appeared as if two young adults were flying quickly across intersections; past empty churches, abandoned buildings and dotted specks of urban renewal.

Yet inside their heads, Elly and Tom felt as if they were in a dream. The world seemed to move in slow motion, as every sound, every shaft of light between brick buildings, each shift of their feet inside their sneakers became amplified. This hypersensitivity was infused by fear. The fear of the inevitable, the unknown, and what was surely to come.

Chapter 10. Lutin

With breathless relief, Elly and Tom finally reached the address of 1 Campus Martius. The winds off of the river seemed to swirl up and around them, as they forced their way through the revolving glass doors of the main floor entrance.

As the children entered the glass atrium, they looked up to see the giant wall of water that rose and fell off of the western wall of the main lobby. The din it created drowned out any quiet conversations that may have been going on between the daily bustling of people in business suits and skirts. Abstract art, like hang gliders of yellow, orange and green hung from the ceiling, giving a soaring, uplifting feel to the entire building. Both of their spirits rose with the lightened atmosphere, allowing them to briefly forget about the heavy words Dr. Beele had shoveled into their heads only moments before.

Elly checked in with security, asking them to dial up her father and let him know that they were in the building. The security officer called up to the Compuware offices and handed Elly the phone. It was her father on the other end, telling Elly that he was running a few minutes late. They were to meet him in the restaurant in 20 minutes.

The Hard Rock Café was located right in same building, along with a number of other shops and galleries. Elly suggested to Tom that they browse around the shops a little bit, before sitting down in the café. Tom agreed, hoping that a little loitering would take his mind off of the Nain Rouge and the dire news that had been delivered that day.

After some shop circling, Elly and Tom decided to enter the bookstore for a few minutes of browsing. Upon entering the clear glass doorway, they both turned toward each other with mutually odd expressions.

"Do you smell that?" Tom asked Elly.

"If you mean that rotten egg, smell, yes, thanks for asking," Elly replied curtly.

"It wasn't me, "Tom retorted, "And I know I've smelled that smell before…"

Then they heard it. That noise, that terrible sound. That low, hissing, laughing, meowing sound... but it was as if no one heard it but them.

Just then, an extremely short and nattily dressed sales clerk approached them. His hair was wiry but well-maintained, his manner cordial and his eyes as black as coal.

"Good day to you," said the man in a low, faint whisper.

"Hello, " the children responded hesitantly.

"I have been expecting you both for some time now." The little man breathed out in a sort of a sigh and rasp combined.

The children stood there stunned.

"Nain Rouge," Elly let the words fly out at the man like a hot coal spit from her charred mouth.

"My name is Lutin, "the little man replied coolly; "And you are impertinent."

Tom instinctively grabbed a hold of Elly's right hand as they both wondered why the Nain Rouge had not attacked them on the spot.

Lutin spoke again, this time in an even quieter tone. "I know that you know who I am. I certainly know who you are. I also know that curator in the museum has shared with you the little he knows about me; the very little, I must say."

Lutin beckoned them back behind a stack of fantasy books, where he could speak with them in even more private. Though

Elly and Tom knew better than to go with this demon, they could not help but be drawn behind the books with him.

Lutin waved his hand and built two short stools out of individual books that stacked themselves upon his command. He did the same for a third, slightly larger stool, upon which he sat, rising just a bit higher than his new audience.

"Since you will soon be mine, I think it only fair that you know the total tale of your unfortunate fate."

Lutin began to tell his version of what Dr. Beele had shared with Elly and Tom:

"I am as old as the land; as old as the river, the trees and everything that grows here. The Native Americans understood this. They respected me, honored me. But then your people came. They scarred the land, cut down the trees, and bridged the river. They bought some land from the natives and then stole away the rest. I attempted to befriend them, I warned them and they laughed at me. I tried to make peace. They wanted war. I told them to stop. They only wanted more. They brought this curse upon themselves."

Elly and Tom noticed Lutin changing color. His peachy flesh was slowly becoming a deep crimson, as his clean-cut, academic veneer peeled away a bit, revealing the seething terror than bubbled just underneath the surface.

Tom could see Lutin's anger growing and quietly interjected, "What is the curse?"

Lutin's voice became more harsh and gravelly, as he continued his story, "They cursed the land with their deeds. The curse is collective, it grows over time. With every act of unkindness, treachery, boorishness, slander, greed, avarice, pride and willful injustice - evil grows."

Elly piped in gently, "Is that the curse then?"

Lutin sat back, less agitated than before. He smiled that horrible smile and spoke with a sickly sweetness, "Evil grows, my child. It grows in me. It is me."

There was a pause of excruciating silence as both children felt flushed and dizzy.

Lutin started in again, "If you really must know the entire story, I will tell you. Your good doctor friend has probably filled you heads with too many lies and falsehoods already. Now, it is time for you to know the truth. It is only fair after all, for it is your story as well. Let me show you."

With that, the dizziness that Elly and Tom had been feeling overcame them. They felt as if they were spinning up and out of the aisle and out the doors of the bookstore.

They were flying. They had no idea how, but they were flying; coasting over tree tops, houses and buildings. In a single thought, they knew that this must be Lutin's magic. He was doing all of this.

Then, just as quickly as they had taken to the air, their bodies slowed and gently settled down on some soft green grass near a flowing river. The landscape was completely unfamiliar to them.

Elly and Tom then heard Lutin's voice penetrate the atmosphere all around them, "Here is your beloved city," Lutin echoed. "Here is where it all started, when the land was fresh, and undefiled."

The disembodied voice pointed them to a group of cabins near the river. It was a small settlement, like the kind they had seen in pictures in their history books.

Without ever speaking, Elly and Tom now realized where they were. Somehow, some way, Lutin had transported them back to Detroit when it was Fort Ponchartrain. They were standing in the year 1701.

"Now, let us go inside that cabin and see what hospitality your kinfolk have in store," the smarmy voice prodded from over their shoulders and around their ears. Almost immediately, the children found themselves inside a small, rustic log cabin. It was clear that through Lutin's dark magic, they could not be seen or heard, even though they could see and hear everything.

Elly and Tom observed six men sitting around a large wooden table. The cabin they were in seemed very rustic indeed. There were a few books set on a side table, a few simple wood-framed beds in opposite corners of the room and almost a dozen wax candles throwing light and shadows against the log walls around them.

The men were talking loudly and drinking wine out of green glass bottles. Their mood seemed to be quite jovial and they seemed to be in high spirits. The children recognized at least one of the men. From their history books, they recognized the face of Antoine de la Mothe Cadillac. They thought that one of the other men might have been Pierre Alphonse de Tonty, but they could not be sure.

Suddenly, Elly and Tom and all of the men at the table heard a terrible wailing outside of the cabin. All the men looked at each with concern. Elly and Tom knew better. They knew whose cry that was and they knew what it meant.

Cadillac stood up, "Open the door and see what that noise is!" he ordered one of his men.

A single man stood up and opened the door. No sooner had it cracked open when a dark shadowy figure, covered with animal fur, spun through the door.

The initial shock of this fantastic entrance faded away into laughter and general merriment from expedition party.

"I seek to speak with the one in charge," said the dirty little man.

One of the men questioned sarcastically, "Who are you, little man of the woods, to demand an audience with anyone?"

The small visitor bowed earnestly and began, "Gentlemen, I come here to you on a mission of peace and diplomacy. You have come here and settled lands for which I am responsible. I come here to work with you, to insure that all of our needs are tended to properly. There is much I have to offer."

There was a brief pause, as Cadillac's men looked around at each other. The amusement had left their faces. In its place was a look of disdain and outrage.

One of the men spoke out roughly, "Why, you impertinent imp! You dare to speak to the great Cadillac in such a manner?! You speak out of turn and far beyond your station. Be gone fool, before I squash you like a bug under my boot!"

Without warning, the man seized the Nain Rouge. The children watched helplessly, as the frustrated dwarf struggled to break free. More men were required to keep hold of the Nain Rouge. Three officers held him tightly, then four, then five. It became increasingly difficult to maintain control of the wild, elfish man. He began biting and gnashing at Cadillac's men, writhing and spinning with growing fury.

"Throw him out!" came the order, shouted by Cadillac.

All of Cadillac's men were yelling back and forth at each other. The Nain Rouge was glowing now, a hot red ember, thrashing and scratching at whomever he could. There was blood, hair and flecks of skin flying into the air. The dust from the clay floor had been spun up into hazy cloud of desperation and confusion.

One of the men managed to open the cabin door. With great effort, all of the soldiers gathered up the whirling mass of anger and rage and threw it out of the cabin and into the night. The door was slammed sharply, then barred and bolted.

An awkward silence now filled the room. Cadillac's men collapsed in exhaustion. All of them were covered with scratches sores, bumps and bruises. One of the men began wrapping his hand with his torn shirt. He had sustained a terrible bite between his thumb and index finger. The wound was bleeding profusely over the clay floor; already his hand was taking on a dark, sickened look.

In this eerie calm after the storm, a hissing voice seeped in, under the cabin door. Though they tried not to listen, Cadillac and all of men heard the low, reptilian words:

"Keep what you steal and steal what you keep
The shepherd must pay for his sins with his sheep."

Then all fell silent.

Elly and Tom were being pulled back. A great suction was vacuuming them out of the cabin and into the air again. They flew backwards, as if a giant rubber band that had been stretched forward as far as it could go was now being snapped back in the opposite direction. Trees, houses and building flew by in a backwards blur.

The children landed with a thud. Slowly but surely, the dizziness subsided and the room came back into focus. Elly and Tom were sitting on the stack of books again. Lutin was sitting directly across from them. It was as if they had never left their seats. He looked at them with a knowing glance, but said nothing about the journey they had just taken. He had wanted them to see with their own eyes, hear with their own ears and feel what really had happened.

"You see," Lutin went on as if without interruption, "I was once upon a time the steward of the land. But I am now, and have been for centuries, the steward of the curse. Each act of evil upon this land resides in me. For many years, there was a balance of good and evil in Detroit; controlling my power; diminishing my presence. But lately, I grow strong. The acts of humanity have erred to the side of wickedness, serving only to feed my insatiable appetite. This cursed land has become my Garden of Eden."

Over the course of this horrible conversation, Lutin became almost giddy in his speech. The manic chortling under his breath served only to unnerve the children even more.

"But why us and why right now?!" Tom blurted out. Lutin calmed himself a bit and looked with great satisfaction upon Elly and Tom, "Why, we are at the tipping point my boy, the tipping point."

Tom asked again, "What do you mean, the tipping point?" Lutin answered, "The tipping point between good and evil. The point where the good of the people is no longer strong enough to hold back the evil that has been building up underneath their feet."

Elly sat up for moment, mustering up what seemed like her last bit of courage, "And what about us then?"

"Oh you," Lutin quipped looking deliciously at both children, "Why, you are the legacy, the ransom that fulfills the curse."

Just then, the children were reminded of the words that had been repeated to them only moments earlier,

"Keep what you steal and steal what you keep
The shepherd must pay for his sins with his sheep."

Tom stepped in again and finally demanded, "Tell us, tell us what is going to happen?!"

Lutin, as if in a delightful trance, breathed in deeply through his nose and simply uttered, "Your deaths will be my rising."

11.

Time and Hour

T<i>here is a</i> primary reaction to danger that resides in all animals, including humans. It is called the "flight-or-flight" response. This reaction is triggered when we sense that a threat is directly upon us. When this happens, we are inclined to either run away or fight for our lives.

Upon absorbing Lutin's words, Elly and Tom felt both; and neither. Tom was inclined to jump off of his stack of books and grab the little man by the throat, choking him into extinction. Elly, on the other hand, was compelled to run; run as fast as she could out of that bookstore.

But instead of a flurry of activity, nothing happened. The children just sat there, frozen. The gravity of what Lutin had revealed had yet to weigh upon them with its full depth and density. The few seconds that past between this awkward trio seemed like hours, as the silence roared in their ears with a dark and powerful emptiness.

It was Lutin who broke the spell of silence with words that flowed out like an incantation, "I must apologize for my bluntness. I can see that I shocked you with what I have revealed. And now, I am sure you look to run away and hide or muster up your remaining crumbs of courage and attack me directly. If either of these things has crossed your mind, I encourage you to let go of such silly schemes. You see, it will not be me who ends your lives; it will be the land."

With a note of rage and frustration, Tom gritted through his clenched teeth, "What the heck is that supposed to mean? How can the land kill us?"

With an air of exasperation, Lutin declared, "My silly boy, did I not tell you that I was the keeper of land, the steward of this region? As steward, I must administer to the business at hand. I am no cheap killer. I am merely the executor of debts that have accrued for centuries. Now the payment has come due."

In a broken, anguished voice, Elly asked, "So, when will it happen, how much time do we have?"

Lutin looked upon the girl with cold satisfaction, "To be

exact my dear, it will be at midnight on July 24th. Now, I imagine that you both are wondering why I know that all these things will occur on that date. If you must know, that is the day that Antoine de la Mothe Cadillac began the settlement of Detroit, over three hundred years ago."

What Lutin had told the children was true. Historical records still exist regarding Antoine de la Mothe Cadillac 's expedition, noting that his party reached the Detroit River on July 23, 1701. At that time, they did not stop in the immediate Detroit area, but rather traveled slightly south to Grosse Ile. He and his men set up camp there and spent the night south of where the city lies today. It was not until the following day, July 24, 1701, that Cadillac's party traveled north on the Detroit River looking for a place to build their settlement. It was at the narrowest part of the river, where the banks were high, that he and his men began construction of Fort Ponchartrain du Detroit.

It was also at that spot where the Nain Rouge first observed the strange, pale creatures, leveling trees and gouging into the land he had sworn to protect.

"Yes," Lutin continued, as if he were bringing simple closure to the entire matter, "That is the day the curse first formed, and it will be the day that the curse comes to fruition ... and I will rule the land once more."

With that, Lutin sat back in quiet satisfaction, reveling in the cold, blank emptiness that hung from Elly and Tom's faces.

12.

The Waiting

Lunch at the Hard Rock Café tasted like ashes and soot. Normally, Elly and Tom relished the upbeat surroundings of music videos, vintage guitars and Detroit rock memorabilia that covered the walls of the restaurant. Elly's dad did not even notice the dreary mood of the two children as they ate their ranch chicken sandwiches will little zeal or interest.

Just think of the situation they were all in; an unemployed father and two children who knew that in a few months, they were going to die. Their predicament seemed terminal.

Elly's dad decided to take the long way home and headed

south down Woodward, all the way to the river. They ended up at Hart Plaza, directly in front of the modern fountain that looked like a giant doughnut propped up on two legs. They turned onto Jefferson Avenue and headed north along the river, past the Renaissance Center, the Winter Garden and the River Walk.

Tom and Elly could not help but feel a twinge of happiness, of slight joy beneath the low hanging clouds. They were overcome with a beautiful sadness. Despite the evil that swirled all around and underneath them, they could still feel flecks of light and hope amid the ever-present shadows. Somehow, these subtle, brilliant glimmers made them feel both optimistic and distraught at the same time. Like the deep, heavy currents of the Detroit River, their stomachs churned with the undertow of emotions that rolled back and forth inside them.

It was as if they were entering in and out of a shadowy tunnel of grief. A back-and-forth cycle of denial, anger, bargaining, depression, and acceptance swirled around inside their heads as they tried to cope with the realization of their own deaths.

As they got back into the car to head back to the suburbs, the grieving process began. Both of them went back and forth, questioning whether any of this had really happened. Maybe it was all a long, drawn-out dream? It all just seemed too implausible, crazy, in fact. They were about to be killed by a red troll in a few months just because some distant ancestor stole his land and kicked him out of town? If they were to tell anyone that, they both would be in therapy for sure. Elly and Tom were in denial. Over the next few days, Elly and Tom spent almost all of their time together. Their conversations shifted from denial to anger, as the realization of their fate became more apparent. What did they do to deserve this? How could they be held accountable for something someone else did hundreds of years ago? Life was not fair.

Once the anger passed, Elly and Tom began to bargain with themselves. Maybe they could pay Lutin off in another way? Maybe if they were better people, did more for others, then their inevitable outcome could change. There had to be a way to avoid the prophecy Lutin had foretold.

But there was no solace in bargaining. After a while, Elly and Tom became depressed with the ever-present thought that they were doomed. The summer that they normally looked forward to all year long had become a dark waiting room of despair. Elly and Tom still made a few trips to the beach, went to a couple of summer concerts and even saw a Tigers baseball game. Though there were moments of excitement and joy, they could not help returning to the overshadowing thought that their time on this earth was waning. Soon, they would be no more.

A shroud of helplessness came over the two children for weeks, as they sat in the darkness of Tom's basement, listening to music, wallowing in the low-volume gloom of unspoken anguish.

It was during one of these basement moping sessions that Tom looked over at Elly and said quietly, "Well El, I guess this is it. In a few weeks, we will be toast."

In a typical grieving process, the final stage is acceptance. It is the time when you accept your fate and tell yourself that you are ready for whatever may come. But for some reason, acceptance would not come. Elly sat there with her arms folded. Her brow was furrowed, as if in great thought or concentration. Tom, on the other hand, lay back with his hands webbed against the back of his head, looking slightly confused. He could not help wondering what the end was going to be like. He just could not wrap his head around the whole idea that in a very short time, he would cease to exist. This one, single thought expanded inside his brain, like a giant soap bubble – spinning and growing futilely until the inevitable "POP!"

Elly readjusted herself on the bed. The deep thoughts that had been etching lines in her face seemed to subside for a moment. She turned her face away from the wall and looked back out into the open room. A new look of determination came across her face. Elly straightened her back, stood up and made direct eye contact with Tom. A new thought was now making its way from her active, excited brain to her waiting, determined lips.

"Tommy, we aren't toast yet… and I have a plan."

Chapter 13. *Revelation*

E*vil lies. It* feeds upon lies. It builds itself up, upon a foundation of distrust, fear, coercion and ego. It moves in shadows, in smoke, in illusion. Evil shrinks and grows within us all and will manifest itself whenever our collective energies accept the darkness as light.

Elly and Tom understood all of this now. It was a matter of life and death that they did. It may not have been fair that they were the ones who had to pay for the sins of their forefathers, but that was their truth now, their reality.

There were only a few weeks left before the 24th of July.

The sightings of the Nain Rouge had become more and more frequent, as news stories and magazine articles chronicled the misdoings and misdeeds of the red dwarf.

Most people still brushed off these increasing occurrences as media hype, superstition or just the general trials and tribulations that were prevalent in a big city. But Elly and Tom knew better. They knew what was going on. They knew that things were bad. They knew things were only going to get worse if they did not do something about it.

The television in the basement murmured in the background. Both children could hear the 5:00pm news stories coming out of the flickering video screen:

"In Detroit today, the mayor has been forced by his constituents to address all of the recent disasters that have befallen the region. During his speech, in front of the 'Spirit of Detroit' statue, Mayor Stuart assured the citizens that he would get to the bottom of things and that law enforcement and high level city officials were working overtime to insure the safety and well-being of city residents.

"In other news, three more water main breaks have been detected in the northwest corner of the city. Violent crime totals have increased 13% since last month and unemployment rates are up 9% since this same time last year..."

"Oh, when will it all end?" Tom mumbled over the television.

"July 24th, unless we do something soon," Elly muttered back.

Tom looked up from his knees, as he cradled his legs in his arms while sitting on the basement floor, "So, what about your plan?"

Elly looked across the room at a blank, paneled wall, "I haven't told you because I was still working some things out, but I'm pretty sure I've got an idea."

"Well, what is it?" Tom prodded.

"I've been thinking about this whole thing," Elly repeated; "This whole thing, everything that's going on, everything that is happening to us, it's all about vengeance; vengeance and energy."

Tom questioned, "What do mean 'energy?'"

Elly continued, "Remember that science project we did last month? About electromagnetic fields and how the earth has its own electromagnetic field?"

"Yeah, so what? What does that have to do with an ancient troll that plans on killing us and reclaiming the city for himself?"

Elly went on, "Listen, I've been doing some research and I think I have found something important." Elly took a hard bound textbook out of her backpack. It was a book about Earth Science. She opened up the book and began to read off of a bookmarked page:

"The earth's natural electromagnetic field has a frequency measured as about 7.8 Hertz. This is

documented in the Schumann Resonance, measured
daily in seismology laboratories.

People give off electromagnetic energy as well,
their brains emitting alpha frequencies of 7 to 9 Hz.
The human brain in a relaxed state will have the same
frequency of vibration as the energy field of the earth."

"You have lost me completely, El," Tom gave in.

Elly sat up and hunched down right next to Tom, face to
face, locking her eyes with his. "Don't you get it? It's all about
energy. It's all about the energy in the earth, the energy we
create. It is all about the bad energy that has been building up
around here for so long. It started with our forefathers and has
been growing ever since.

"We are either in harmony or in discord with the land.
Science has proven that when we are at the same frequency
as the earth's energy field, we're at peace and happy. But when
we do bad things and create bad energy, the earth responds
negatively.

"Lutin is tied to the land, he said so. He's the tipping point.
He is the incarnation of bad energy, of evil!"

Tom's eyes registered with Elly. He finally understood
everything she had said. He even understood her plan, though
she had yet to even tell him.

"Release the energy," Tom whispered in blinking revelation,

"We need to release the evil. We need to bring the harmony and balance back to the way it was before our relatives started this whole mess."

Elly put her forehead against Tom's forehead and squeezed his shoulder gently, "Yes, Tom, we need to get Lutin off the land, somehow. It won't be easy, but I think it can be done. It will be like pulling a plug from a socket."

Tom breathed deeply, 'Yeah, as long as we don't get electrocuted first...."

Chapter **14.** *Subterfuge*

The **Windsor-Detroit** International Freedom Festival was in full swing.

The Windsor-Detroit International Freedom Festival is recognized and respected as the best Festival that represents the peace, unity, freedom, and friendship shared between Canada and the United States. The festival combines Independence Day and Canada Day, and lasts several weeks in July, culminating in a spectacular fireworks display over the Detroit River.

Along with hundreds of thousands of other people from the area, Elly and Tom always enjoyed the freedom festival. This was a time of year when Detroit could celebrate its freedom with its international neighbor across the river, Canada. It was a chance for their families to get together and go downtown for all of the festival events. Tom loved to meet up with his friends at the Techno Music Fest, where he could listen to the latest techno sounds and meet people from all over the world.

Elly, on the other hand, preferred the food festivals, where she could sample foods from many different countries, while joining in the dancing and parades from cultures around the globe.

Of course, the most fun of all was the night of the fireworks. Both sides of the Detroit River were always filled with excited spectators, waiting anxiously for nightfall and the largest fireworks display in North America.

However, this year was not the same. Everything was different.

It was the perfect opportunity for Lutin to wreak havoc upon the city and drag his cloak of darkness completely over the region. Tom and Elly did not even want to go downtown this year, but they knew that they had to. They had to be there just in case anything bad should happen. And they knew that it would. In fact, they were counting on it.

On the evening of the fireworks, Tom and Elly decided to meet on Jefferson Avenue, by the "Joe Louis Fist" statue. This location put them right near the riverfront and directly in the middle of all the action and excitement. If Lutin was going to make trouble, this would surely be the spot where he would do it.

Lutin had been causing trouble throughout the week of the festival. Tents had fallen down, porta-johns had been tipped over and garbage had been inadvertently tossed around the festival grounds. City officials had blamed a bunch of trouble-making teenagers, but Elly and Tom knew better. They also knew it would get worse. That is why Elly's plan had to be simple and direct.

The plan was two-fold; find Lutin and lead him into their trap. Finding him would not be a problem, fooling him would be a whole different story.

Elly and Tom needed to expect the unexpected.

The city was abuzz with energy. The smell of coney dogs, bottle rockets and fried elephant ears filled the air, mingling with the warm wind off of the water and the faint saxophone hum of a jazz musician on the main stage at Hart Plaza.

Elly and Tom stood by the "Fist" statue, scanning the crowd for anything suspicious.

"Do you feel different?" Elly turned to Tom as their eyes watched the crowd, moving back and forth like heads at a tennis match.

Tom answered, "Different? What do you mean?"

"I can't quite explain it," Elly continued, "I just feel drained. I feel kind of weak, emotionless… like my soul is sick."

Tom thought about it for a minute, "Yeah, I think I know what you mean. Here we are, knowing that we are doomed in a few days and somehow, it really doesn't seem to matter."

"I think it's the city. I noticed that these feelings get worse when we come down here," Elly stated quite factually.

Just then, the children heard it. That sickly, high-pitched siren sound. They looked around to see if anyone else in the crowd had noticed or reacted. No one did. They were the only ones who had heard it.

It was Lutin. He was near them, somewhere in the sea of spectators, he was hiding.

The faint wailing was growing louder. Elly and Tom had the urge to cover their ears but resisted, not wanting to draw attention to themselves.

"Hello children…" came a slithery sweet voice from behind them. Tom and Elly turned around to see a shortish, plain-looking balloon vendor staring up at them.

"Enjoying the festival?" the balloon vendor quipped with a knowing grin.

"Not as much as we could be," Tom replied coldly.

Night was falling slowly upon the city as the three figures stood in a miniature triangle, exchanging words, while the rest of the crowd sizzled with the excitement of the impending fireworks.

"You two don't look so well," Lutin questioned, "Are you feeling a little down lately?"

Elly was the first to reply, "Not that it's any of your business, but yes, Tom and I have not been feeling all that great – ever since we ran into you!"

Lutin made a few slight clicking sounds with his tongue in mock sympathy. "Well, not to worry my friends, it will all be over soon. By midnight tomorrow, all of your troubles will be over."

Their stomachs churned, as the sinking feeling of their fates returned. The freedom festival had taken their minds off of their worries for a little while. But now, the gravity of the situation had returned with a weight and intensity that seemed so much heavier than before.

Tom growled at Lutin under his breath, "So, how are you going to do it?"

"Do what?" Lutin returned a false, puzzled look to Tom.

Elly jumped in, "You know what he means. How are you going to destroy us?"

"Destroy you?" Lutin shot back with dramatic, false indignation, "Why, I told you before, I am no killer.

"But I suppose I can share with you the means by which you both shall part from this earth," Lutin confided. "Ironically, it has already begun. The change, the strange way that you both have been feeling, that, my children, is the beginning of the end. Your lives will not end as abruptly as you might have thought – or even as you might have wished. No, the curse that you were born into has taken these many years to come to fruition. It is a slow, absorbing curse that envelops you over time. That is why, by tomorrow evening, the Elly and Tom that the world has known for the past 13 years will simply fade away – disappear forever."

The children were silent. What else could they say? Their fates had been sealed.

Lutin broke the silence with an awkward giggling, "Oh, let's not be so gloomy. Cheer up, the fireworks are about to start!"

Lutin was right. Darkness had fallen completely around them. Within the shadowy water of the river, barges had been anchored as platforms for launching the giant mortars that would soon send rainbows of sparks and fire into the air.

Within seconds of their awareness, the spectacle of lights and sounds began overhead. It seemed as if the entire world was cheering, as the first rocket of red, blue and orange exploded high over the water.

Lutin leaned over casually to Elly and Tom, barely able to yell over the noise of the crowd and fireworks, "I know what will lift your spirits… perhaps if I brought the show a little bit closer… so you can both see better…"

He made a small gesture with his hand.

Suddenly the fireworks stopped and people could be heard booing and complaining all around them.

Then, voices near the river began shouting, "The barge! The barge! The barge is off its mooring! Get away from the shore! Get away from the shore!"

Elly and Tom whipped around and faced Lutin. He was snickering under his breath and moving his hand in a sweeping motion.

"What have you done?!" Tom yelled at him.

"I am doing you a favor. Don't you want to see the show up close?"

The trail of a blue fireball whizzed over their heads. The crowd was rushing away from the shore, screaming and pushing to get out of the way of the flaming missiles that were being shot, perpendicular across Jefferson Avenue.

"Stop it! Stop it now!" Elly grabbed Lutin, screaming. As quickly as the chaos started, it stopped. The barge that had floated so close to shore began moving back into the middle of the river.

Lutin spoke softly, "I am so sorry that you did not appreciate my kind gesture. In fact, I am a bit hurt."

Elly, still full of adrenaline and anger, shot back, "Kind gesture? Are you kidding me? The only ones really hurt are those people in the crowd!"

Lutin furrowed his brow and retorted, "Should I begin the show again, even closer this time?"

"No!" both Elly and Tom shouted.

"Well, why shouldn't I? What do I care about the welfare of strangers? " Lutin asked with a coy, casual smile.

Tom stated as firmly as he could, "Don't do it Lutin. More people could get injured, or worse. Besides, you already have us, what more do you want?"

"Not much more," was Lutin's response.

Elly and Tom looked at each other nervously.

Lutin continued, "All I ask is that you allow me the pleasure of your company in your final hours."

Tom replied, "What are you getting at?"

"It is quite simple, my boy. I want to watch you die, both of you."

As if by intuition or choreography, Elly and Tom bent over at the waist, holding their stomachs in gut-wrenching pain. It was as if Lutin's words were daggers, shredding the very fibers of their beings, weakening their draining spirits.

Elly averted Lutin's black eyes and asked, "Why? Why can't you just let it happen? Let us pass on and be done with it."

Lutin licked his lips avariciously, as if he had been waiting for that question for hundreds of years, "Oh my sweet, revenge is best served cold and I intend to savor the taste of my victory. Watching the two of you wither away into nothingness, while

I rise in triumph, well, that is a meal in which I have longed to partake. So, I am willing to spare a few of your human brethren in order that I might dine with you in your last moments on earth."

Elly and Tom were quiet for a very long time. The crowd of people had settled down and returned slowly to their blankets and folding chairs down by the river. The fireworks soon began again, without incident. The children regained their composure and sat on the soft grass of the boulevard between Jefferson Avenue. Lutin stood there, staring at them with anxious anticipation, waiting for their answer.

Elly and Tom appeared empty and broken. They sat there, heads hung between their knees with faces drooped, like melted candle wax. Lutin never moved or wavered. He just stood there, staring, waiting patiently for their response.

The answer finally came, "Yes," was the one word answer that came from both Elly and Tom.

Lutin's face lit up slightly, shining in the pyrotechnic glow that strobed over their heads. "Lovely, my dears, lovely. I look forward to seeing you both tomorrow evening. Until then, I bid you a fond adieu."

With that, Lutin disappeared in a tiny fog of sulphuric smoke, mingling with the rest of the fireworks that filled the evening air. His high-pitched cackle could be heard fading in their ears, like a distant emergency siren, warning of a far-off, approaching storm.

Tom breathed deeply and whispered to Elly, "Well, I guess this is it."

Elly turned her face to him and calmly replied, "Yup, he's fallen right into our trap."

Chapter 15

Darkness Before Dawn

The *final event* of the International Freedom Festival was to be held at the Michigan State Fairgrounds on the northern border of Detroit. The fairgrounds rested alongside Woodward Avenue to the north and south, and Eight Mile Road to the east and west. This would be the last big event at the old auditorium, arena and midway. The money had run out that kept the fairground up and running. Large billboarded FOR SALE signs had already been hammered into the ground in front of the main entry; another sad sign of how bad things had gotten.

The fairgrounds were old. Over one hundred years old, to

be exact. Joseph L. Hudson, founder of a Detroit area leading department store Hudson's, gave the State Fair its permanent home and formed the State Fair Land Company in October, 1904. By February 28, 1905, this company, through three separate transactions, had acquired the land between 7 1/2 and 8 Mile Roads, east of Woodward Avenue. The area was truly rural then, farmland some seven miles from Detroit's City Hall and far beyond the populated streets of the city.

Now, it soon would all be only a distant memory. This center of civic and state pride would shortly be returned to its rural state, filled only with crabgrass, weeds, wildflowers and the faded cheers, shrieks and shouts of excited fairgoers, crying out like ghosts from a century gone by.

Elly and Tom woke up late on the morning of the 23th. Neither of them wanted to get out of bed. After the night they had been through, both children felt as if they had run a 20K marathon, weak, tired and out of breath. Ever since Lutin had come into their lives, they had grown weary. No one could tell that there had been a change in them. Oh, their parents had mentioned that they looked thinner or a bit tired, but everyone was so busy with their own problems, that they failed to see that Elly and Tom's souls were slowly leeching out of them.

The day dragged on, as the cool morning sun burned into a hazy, humid afternoon. Despite their fatigue, Elly and Tom agreed to stick to the plan, they had to, it was their only choice –

their only chance. By late afternoon, they were ready to take the bus down Woodward to the fairgrounds. The plan was to have dinner down at the fair, ride the rides, see the attractions and wait for Lutin to show up.

The bus ride to the fairgrounds was uneventful. Elly and Tom watched the buildings pass; old churches, the used bookstore, and numerous gas stations and fast food restaurants. The last thing they saw before they came to the fairground stop was Woodlawn Cemetery. The children used to play a superstitious game when passing a cemetery. They used to close their eyes and hold their breath until the vehicle they were in had completely passed the graveyard. The rule was that if you breathed or open your eyes before you passed the cemetery, you would die. This time it wasn't a game, for the breath they were holding could be their last.

The hydraulic brakes hissed as the bus came to a complete stop. The children open their eyes and looked out of the window. Woodlawn Cemetery had disappeared onto the other side of the street. In its place, the Michigan State Fairgrounds loomed large in front of them. They had reached their final destination.

The evening sky cooled with the setting of the summer sun. Pale blue was replaced with the violet orange of the emerging darkness that filtered through warm and busy air. Elly and Tom felt completely out of place. The curse upon them had taken its toll, and it took almost all of their energy to make their way into the fairgrounds. They both wished that they could just curl up in a ball in a dark, quiet room. But here they were, amid the lights, noise and maddening activity of carnival games, Tilt-a-Whirls, and an electric, slow-spinning Ferris wheel.

As Elly and Tom trudged passed a Skee-Ball tent, they heard a familiar yowling, like the cry of a tomcat.

"Hello, my friends, "came a slippery, frothy voice from behind them.

The children turned around to see Lutin. He was formally dressed from head to toe in a tuxedo with tails, complete with top hat and cane. He could have easily been mistaken for a ring-master, blending right in with the rest of the festival performers.

"I thought, since this was a special occasion, I should dress appropriately," Lutin quipped with a devilish smile.

Elly and Tom were speechless. They could feel themselves growing weaker and weaker as they ambled aimlessly around the fairgrounds.

"Why not take a ride on the Ferris wheel?" Lutin goaded them, "I mean, it is your last night on this earth; why not enjoy yourselves a little?"

Without really knowing, Elly and Tom found themselves rising up above the midway on the giant Ferris wheel. Lutin sat between them, on the top of the car, dangling his little legs wistfully over the edge of seat.

"So, what does it feel like, little ones? To know that, in a few moments, you will be no more?"

"What do you care?" Tom shot back.

"Oh, I care very much, "Lutin replied, "I cannot tell you how much I am enjoying watching you two, slowly wither away. I have waited over 300 years for retribution and I want to savor this taste, this flavor for as long as possible."

"You really are w-wicked," Elly weakly stammered.

"That fact," Lutin admitted, "I have never denied. But you must remember, it is you and your kind that fed me, nurtured me, groomed me with your lies, distrust, greed, violence, and anger. Humankind empowered me and made me what I am today. And for that, I thank you."

The Ferris wheel came to a slow stop and Elly and Tom stumbled awkwardly out of their car. It was very near midnight and both children felt completely empty. No one seemed to notice that they were being slowly drained of life right in the middle of the midway. An odd, out-of-body feeling came over them.

Tom remembered attending the wake they had for his great aunt. He remembered the casket in the corner, the people with drawn faces, whispering, mumbling all the while ignoring the cold body that lay motionless at one end of the room. Tom felt like that body; an empty shell.

Elly was drowning. Drowning in a sea of darkness, surrounded by the joy and happiness of festival goers, moving passed her with careless purpose. She could only feel the shiver of black water filling her lungs, dousing the diminishing light of her spirit.

"We have to get out of here," Elly cried softly as she took Tom's hand.

"OK, let's make it quick," Tom croaked with a hollow voice.

Lutin had never left. He had been standing right there, all along, watching the two disintegrate before his eyes.

"Oh, and where do we think we are going?" Lutin questioned delightfully.

"We need to get some air," they both said in unison.

Tom and Elly stumbled across the midway. There legs felt like they had lead weights in their shoes. Their arms felt as if they were filled with heavy, wet sand. They tried to hide for just a moment. Then without warning, both of them collapsed behind one of the concession tents.

"Tom, I don't think I can make it," Elly sighed.

"Oh Elly, come on, it's only a little bit further. We can't let him win, we just can't!" Tom pleaded.

Just then, the children felt a warm hand on both of their shoulders. It was not Lutin, it couldn't be. This touch felt warm and reassuring, not cold, empty and evil like the Nain Rouge. Tom and Elly looked up from their hands and knees to see one of the carnival workers staring down at them. He was dressed in festive garb, complete with a multi-colored suit, covered with bright bows, fancy buttons, assorted pins and a large, flowered boutonnière. There was something very familiar about this man but Tom and Elly could not quite figure out from where they knew him.

Quietly, the man spoke to them, "Children, listen to me – I know what you are up against. You can't give up now. We are all counting on you."

As the man spoke, Tom and Elly noticed a familiar medallion hanging, almost invisible, from the man's lapel. There was an image of a knight, slaying a green dragon on it. They read the words wrapped around the outer edge of the knight's banner, "Honi soit qui mal y pense…"

Elly looked over at Tom and whispered, "The Order of the Garter!"

The children looked up at the man again and suddenly, all was revealed. "Dr. Beele!" they both yelled.

"Yes," Dr. Beele shushed them; "It is me. I have been following you for some time now. It is imperative that you both keep moving. I have faith in you. I have distracted Lutin just enough to give you a fighting chance to defeat him."

It was true. Dr. Beele had diverted Lutin's attention only minutes before, coercing him into playing a game of chance at one of the other gaming tents.

Dr. Beele continued, "Time is short, you must go. It is all up

to you now. Just remember, it is always darkest before the dawn
– and you are not alone..."

With that, the children held each other, got up and moved
as quickly as they could off of the midway and out of the
fairgrounds.

"Don't hurry on my account!" Lutin suddenly reappeared
behind Tom and Elly. His voice was filled with sarcastic glee as
he chided them from behind.

Elly and Tom exited the fair and scurried, stumbling along
the way down Eight Mile Road. Lutin followed them with ease,
dancing around the two singing,

"Keep what you steal and steal what you keep
The shepherd must pay for his sins with his sheep!"

The two children held each even closer and ran across the
intersection. Once they had reached the other side, they turned
to face Lutin.

The clock at the fairgrounds began the first strikes of midnight. Unconsciously, Elly and Tom began counting the chimes
in their heads.

ONE.

"So," Lutin spoke, a bit winded from his dance, "how does it
feel to die?"

TWO.

"How does it feel to know it is all over?"

THREE.

"How does it feel to know that all you have ever worked for and dreamed about is gone?"

FOUR.

"Why don't you answer?"

FIVE.

"Are you afraid to die?"

SIX.

Elly straightened up, finally willing to address Lutin directly, "Are you asking if we are afraid to die?"

SEVEN.

"Yes," Lutin grinned feverishly, "Are You Afraid To Die?"

The answer came back, "No, are you?"

At that moment, Elly and Tom straightened up. They appeared to have regained a little of their strength. In a single motion, Tom boosted Elly up a pole that held the street signs. Elly reached up and slowly swiveled the two signs that read "Woodward Avenue" and 'Eight Mile Road" back to their original positions.

EIGHT.

"What have you done?!" Lutin howled, as his skin flushed red as fire.

NINE.

Elly, still out of breath, replied, "It's not what we did, it's what you did. You crossed the line."

TEN.

Tom added with equal breathlessness, "You thought you were headed west, when you were headed north. So much for being in touch with the land. You're out of your territory, Lutin."

ELEVEN.

"You crossed the line, Lutin," Elly said again.

Tom chimed in, "You left the city."

The Nain Rouge was glowing red now; screaming in a horribly, screeching wail - spinning madly, out of control.

Elly and Tom were regaining more of their strength. They could feel the life coming back into their bodies. A confident, secure warmth flooded over them, as their spirits re-ignited, bringing the color and glow back to their faces.

Lutin continued to spin and shout, faster and louder, screaming with a rage that echoed over hundreds of years, pulsating red and orange into the night time sky.

Elly and Tom covered their ears, shielding themselves from the destructive decibels being shot from Lutin's flaming, gaping mouth.

TWELVE.

An explosion erupted on the spot where Lutin had been whirling and gyrating. The force of the explosion was so strong, that it knocked Elly and Tom back down, onto the ground. Lutin was gone.

All that was left was a black, oily puddle on the sidewalk that reeked of sulphur and mineral spirits. Both of the children watched in exhaustion as the greasy, dark slick slid off of the sidewalk and down, out of sight, into a waiting sewer drain.

"Your plan, it worked," Tom said with breathless exuberance.

"Yes," Elly gasped, "I almost can't believe it. I knew that something good would happen if we could just get him outside of the city limits – like pulling a plug from a socket."

Their plan had worked. Elly and Tom had figured out the source of Lutin's power. As Steward of the Straits, the Nain Rouge was tied into the land. He drew his strength and power from the energy of the land on which Detroit was founded.

But the source of his power was also the source of his weakness. For Tom and Elly had guessed, and guessed rightly, that Lutin could not exist apart from his land. If he were to step off of his claimed territory, he would lose all of his power. And when he crossed north over Eight Mile Road, he unplugged his own power cord.

Tom and Elly had taken a big chance. Thank goodness they had guessed right.

Lutin was no more.

Elly and Tom got back on their feet, feeling better than they had in weeks. The light had come back into their eyes and the rosiness of life now blushed their cheeks once more. Though their legs were still a little wobbly from their recent battle, Elly and Tom had returned to the world of the living.

Awkwardly holding hands, they both made their way back across the intersection to the fairgrounds. The lights from the fair twinkled into the night, like little beacons of hope amidst the inky black all around them.

The night was no longer restless. It was peaceful. The stars, that once appeared veiled and muted, now shown so brightly in the sky, that it almost seemed like dawn.

The fair was closing. It was time to go home.

Epilogue.

E*lly woke in* the morning as if it had all been a dream; the museum, the festival, the state fairgrounds. She got out of bed feeling fatigued but happy, like after working all day in her mom's garden.

As she went downstairs for breakfast, she heard her dad in the kitchen, already busy making breakfast. He seemed to be more cheerful than he had been for the past few weeks. Elly even thought she heard him whistling under his breath.

"Guess what?" were her father's first words of the morning.

"I don't know, what?" Elly replied sleepily.

"They called me back to work. I start on Monday."

A smile came across Elly's face. It was the first time she had smiled in weeks.

After breakfast, Elly stopped over at Tom's house. Tom was helping his mom clean out the front study, making way for her new home office.

"Hey Elly, come on in," Tom said when he saw Elly at the front door. "I'm helping my mom get ready for her new business."

"That sounds great, did she get a new job?" Elly asked.

"Well, sort of," Tom replied. 'She's setting up her own photography business. She has a web site and everything. She even has four clients already! Now she can be her own boss. The front study is going to be her new office."

"That is really cool - oh, my dad got called back to work too." Elly responded.

"Well, I guess things are looking up for everybody," Tom observed as he lugged another box of file folders into the front study.

"Yeah, things sure seem different since last night," said Elly in a thoughtful tone, "I think what we did outside of the state fairgrounds is already making a difference."

Tom gave Elly a "be quiet" look as his mom passed by on her way upstairs. With that, they both went out to the front porch to talk. While sitting there they noticed that things did seem different; different in a better way. It was as if hope had trickled back into their lives, little drops at a time, falling into a well that had for so long been empty.

After just sitting there for awhile, Tom spoke up, "So El, how long do you think this will last, the good stuff, I mean?"

Elly was quiet. She leaned back against the porch step, pondering his question. After a long, thoughtful pause, she replied,

"I don't know, Tommy. In a lot of ways, I think may be up to us. I guess the good stuff lasts long as we want it to..."

The End.

8690124R0

Made in the USA
Charleston, SC
05 July 2011